# Index

The Boy Who Turned Himself
  into a Peanut  26
The Dog and the Bone  12
The Gingerbread Boy  14
The Hare and the Turtle  35
Henny-Penny  42
The History of an Apple Pie  25
The House That Jack Built  30
The Lion and the Mouse  62
The Little Red Hen  52
Little Red Riding Hood  36
The Princess and the Pea  20
The Three Bears  6
The Three Billy Goats Gruff  48
The Three Little Pigs  56
The Wind and the Sun  46

D1364036

One day the lion was walking through the forest when suddenly some hunters captured him with a net.

The lion roared his loudest roar.

The trees shook, but the net stayed as strong as ever.

Far away the mouse heard the roar.

He ran to the lion and nibbled at the net. He nibbled and nibbled until he made a big hole in the net.

The lion squeezed through the hole and walked away with the mouse at his side.

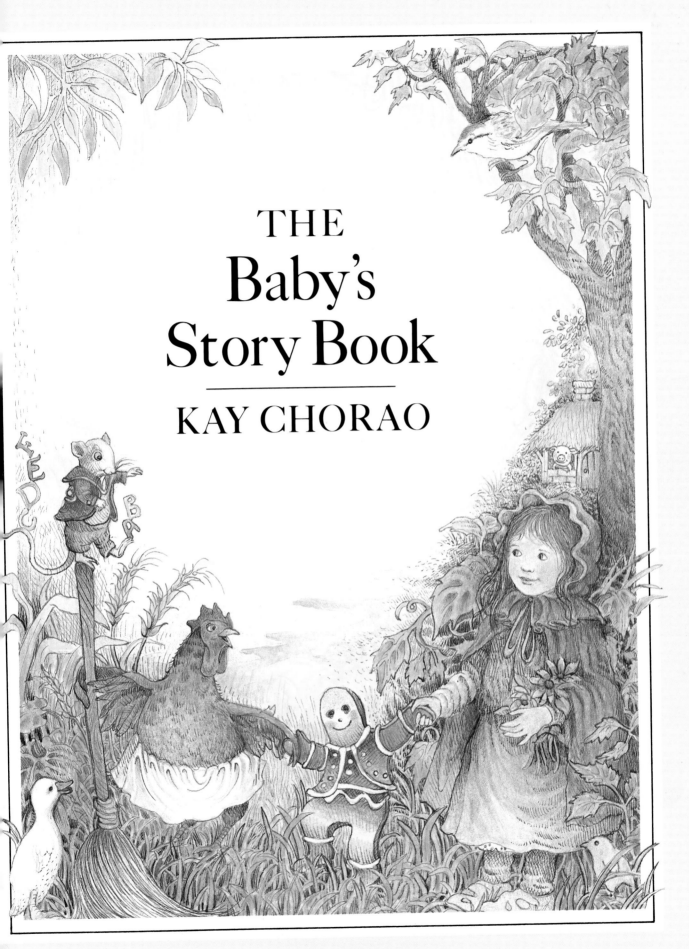

# THE
# Baby's
# Story Book

## KAY CHORAO

A Puffin Unicorn

PUFFIN UNICORN BOOKS

Published by the Penguin Group
Penguin Books USA Inc., 375 Hudson Street,
New York, New York 10014, U.S.A.
Penguin Books Ltd, 27 Wrights Lane, London W8 5TZ, England
Penguin Books Australia Ltd, Ringwood, Victoria, Australia
Penguin Books Canada Ltd, 10 Alcorn Avenue, Toronto,
Ontario, Canada M4V 3B2
Penguin Books (N.Z.) Ltd, 182-190 Wairau Road,
Auckland 10, New Zealand
Penguin Books Ltd, Registered Offices:
Harmondsworth, Middlesex, England

Unicorn is a registered trademark of Dutton Children's Books,
a division of Penguin Books USA Inc.
Library of Congress number 84-26005
ISBN 0-14-055738-5
Published in the United States by Dutton Children's Books,
a division of Penguin Books USA Inc.
Editor: Ann Durell   Designer: Riki Levinson
Printed in Hong Kong by South China Printing Co.
First Puffin Unicorn Edition 1995
1 3 5 7 9 10 8 6 4 2

THE BABY'S STORY BOOK is also available in hardcover from
Dutton Children's Books.

This book belongs to

_____

# Contents

The Three Bears  6

The Dog and the Bone  12

The Gingerbread Boy  14

The Princess and the Pea  20

The History of an Apple Pie  25

The Boy Who Turned Himself
   into a Peanut  26

The House That Jack Built  30

The Hare and the Turtle  35

Little Red Riding Hood  36

Henny-Penny  42

The Wind and the Sun  46

The Three Billy Goats Gruff  48

The Little Red Hen  52

The Three Little Pigs  56

The Lion and the Mouse  62

Index of Titles  64

## The Three Bears

Once upon a time, there were three bears. One was a little wee Baby Bear. One was a middle-sized Mama Bear. And one was a great big Papa Bear.

Each bear had a bowl for porridge and a chair to sit on and a bed to sleep in. Baby Bear had a little wee bowl and a little wee chair and a little wee bed. Mama Bear had a middle-sized bowl and a middle-sized chair and a middle-sized bed. Papa Bear had a great big bowl and a great big chair and a great big bed.

One day the three bears took a walk while their porridge cooled on the table.

A little girl named Goldilocks passed by the house and looked in the window.

She could see that no one was home. So she lifted the latch on the door and walked inside.

Right away she saw the porridge cooling on the table. And she decided to have some.

First she tasted Papa Bear's porridge, but it was too hot. Next she tasted Mama Bear's porridge, but it was too cold. Then she tasted Baby Bear's porridge, and it was just right. So she ate it all up.

Then Goldilocks sat on the great big chair, but it was too hard. She tried the middle-sized chair, but it was too soft. So she tried the little wee chair, and it was just right. But she rocked it so hard that it broke, and she fell to the floor.

Goldilocks picked herself up and went upstairs. There she found three beds. First she lay down on the great big bed, but that was too high. Next she lay down on the middle-sized bed, but that was too low. So Goldilocks lay down on the little wee bed. It was just right. She fell fast asleep.

When the three bears returned from their walk, they sat down to have their porridge.

Papa Bear looked at his bowl. "SOMEONE HAS BEEN EATING MY PORRIDGE!" he roared in his great big voice.

"Someone has been eating my porridge," said Mama Bear in her middle-sized voice.

Baby Bear looked in his bowl. "Someone has been eating my porridge and has eaten it all up!" he cried in his little wee voice.

"SOMEONE HAS BEEN SITTING ON MY CHAIR," said Papa Bear in his great big voice.

"Someone has been sitting in my chair," said Mama Bear in her middle-sized voice.

"Someone has been sitting in my chair, and it's all broken!" cried Baby Bear in his little wee voice.

The bears thought they should look upstairs.

Papa Bear looked at his bed. "SOMEONE HAS BEEN LYING IN MY BED," he roared in his great big voice.

Mama Bear looked at her bed. "Someone has been lying in my bed, too," she said in her middle-sized voice.

Baby Bear looked at his bed. "Someone has been lying in my bed, and here she IS!" he cried.

Goldilocks woke up. When she saw the three bears, she jumped up, ran down the stairs and out the front door. She ran all the way home. And the three bears never saw Goldilocks again.

## The Dog and the Bone

A dog one day stole a bone.

He ran and he ran with it.

He ran until he reached a bridge over a clear stream.

The dog looked down into the water and saw his own reflection.

Who is that dog with the nice big bone? he asked himself.

He growled. The dog in the water growled too.

I want that bone. It looks bigger than mine, he thought.

He snarled. The dog in the water snarled too.

Then he opened his mouth and made a grab for the other dog's bone.

But when he opened his mouth, his bone fell into the stream and disappeared.

That day the dog had nothing to eat.

# The Gingerbread Boy

Once upon a time, a little old man and a little old woman lived all alone. They wanted to have a child, so they decided to make one out of gingerbread. They mixed the dough and rolled out a gingerbread boy and popped him in the oven.

When the gingerbread boy was finished baking, they opened the oven and out he hopped.

"Run, run, as fast as you can. You can't catch me! I'm the gingerbread man!" he said.

The little old woman and the little old man ran after the gingerbread boy, but they could not catch him.

On and on ran the gingerbread boy until he came to a cow.

"Stop," said the cow, "I want to eat you."

But the gingerbread boy said, "I have run away from a little old woman and a little old man, and I can run away from you too. I can, I can!"

The cow chased the gingerbread boy, but she couldn't catch him.

"Run, run, as fast as you can. You can't catch me! I'm the gingerbread man!" he cried.

Soon he came to a horse.

"Please stop, little gingerbread boy," said the horse. "I want to eat you."

The gingerbread boy did not stop. He said, "I have run away from a cow and a little old woman and a little old man, and I can run away from you too. I can, I can!"

The horse chased the gingerbread boy.

"Run, run, as fast as you can. You can't catch me! I'm the gingerbread man!"

And the horse couldn't catch him.

The gingerbread boy ran on until he reached a field full of farmers.

"Stop so we can eat you," said the farmers.

But the gingerbread boy didn't stop. "I have run away from a horse, a cow, and a little old woman and a little old man, and I can run away from you too. I can, I can!"

The farmers ran, but the gingerbread boy ran faster.

"Run, run as fast as you can. You can't catch me! I'm the gingerbread man!"

By and by he came to a fox sitting on a riverbank.

The gingerbread boy ran past the fox. "I have run away from a field full of farmers, a horse, a cow, and a little old woman and a little old man, and I can run away from you too. I can, I can! You can't catch me! I'm the gingerbread man!"

The fox smiled and said, "I do not want to catch you. I will help you run away. Hop on my back and I will help you cross this river."

The gingerbread boy hopped on the fox's tail, and the fox began to swim.

"You are too heavy on my tail," said the fox. "Jump on my back."

The gingerbread boy did.

The fox swam a little farther, then he said, "I am afraid you will get wet on my back. Jump on my shoulder."

So the gingerbread boy did.

The fox swam on. Then he said, "Oh, dear, my shoulder is sinking. Jump on my nose, and I will hold you out of the water."

The gingerbread boy hopped onto the fox's nose, and snip-snap, the fox opened and closed his strong jaws. And that was the end of the gingerbread boy.

# The Princess and the Pea

Once upon a time, there was a prince who wanted to find a princess to marry. But she would have to be a *real* princess.

He searched and searched. He met one princess after another, but there was always something the matter. They just weren't real princesses. So at last he returned home without a wife.

One night there was a terrible storm. The lightning flashed, the thunder roared, and the rain fell down in buckets.

In the midst of all this noise and rain, someone knocked at the palace gate. The old king himself went to open the gate, and when he pushed it open, he found a young woman.

"I am a princess. May I come in?" she asked.

The king looked at her. She was dripping wet and looked a terrible sight. The king did not quite believe that she was a princess, but he let her in anyway.

The queen gave her dry clothing and offered her a bed for the night. I'll find out if she's a real princess, the queen said to herself. And she placed a tiny pea beneath the mattress. Then she placed twenty mattresses on top of that, and twenty down comforters on top of that.

The girl carefully climbed onto her tall, swaying bed, and tried to fall asleep.

The next morning the queen asked her, "How did you sleep?"

"I didn't sleep a wink! Heaven knows what was in that bed. I feel as though I'd been lying on a rock. I'm black and blue from head to toe."

The king and queen and the prince were pleased. At last they had found a real princess. Otherwise she could never have felt that tiny pea through twenty mattresses and twenty down comforters. Only a real princess could be that sensitive.

So, there was a royal wedding, and the prince and princess lived happily ever after.

# The History of an Apple Pie

## written by Z

A  Apple Pie!

B  bit it.

C  cried for it.

D  danced for it.

E  eyed it.

F  fiddled for it.

G  gobbled it.

H  hid it.

I  inspected it.

J  jumped over it.

K  kicked it.

L  laughed at it.

M  mourned for it.

N  nodded for it.

O  opened it.

P  peeped into it.

Q  quaked for it.

R  rode for it.

S  skipped for it.

T  took it.

U  upset it.

V  viewed it.

W  warbled for it.

Xerxes drew his sword for it.

Y  yawned for it.

Z, zealous that all good boys and girls
   should be acquainted with his family,
   sat down and wrote the history of it.

## The Boy Who Turned Himself
## into a Peanut

One day a little boy decided to fool his father. "I will hide myself so well that you will not be able to find me," he said.

"Hide wherever you like," said the father. "I will just go home now and take a rest."

So the boy looked for a hiding place.

He saw a peanut that had three kernels, so he turned himself into one of the kernels and hid in the peanut.

Just then a rooster came along and swallowed the peanut.

Then a wild bush cat leaped on the rooster and swallowed him.

Then a dog saw the bush cat and, after a long chase, gobbled him down.

The dog was sleeping when a python slithered by and made a meal of him.

The python went down to the river and was caught in a fish trap.

Meanwhile, the father had finished resting and was looking everywhere for his son. Not seeing him, he walked to the river to inspect his fish trap.

There he found a large python, which he opened and found a dog. He opened the dog and found a bush cat. He opened the bush cat and found a rooster. He opened the rooster and found a peanut.

Of course, when he opened the peanut, out jumped his son!

The boy was so surprised to be found that he never tried to fool his father again.

## The House That Jack Built

This is the house that Jack built.

This is the malt
That lay in the house that Jack built.

This is the rat
That ate the malt,
That lay in the house that Jack built.

This is the cat
That killed the rat,
That ate the malt,
That lay in the house that Jack built.

This is the dog
That worried the cat,
That killed the rat,
That ate the malt,
That lay in the house that Jack built.

This is the cow with the crumpled horn
That tossed the dog,
That worried the cat,
That killed the rat,
That ate the malt,
That lay in the house that Jack built.

This is the maiden all forlorn

That milked the cow with the crumpled horn,

That tossed the dog,

That worried the cat,

That killed the rat,

That ate the malt,

That lay in the house that Jack built.

This is the man all tattered and torn

That kissed the maiden all forlorn,

That milked the cow with the crumpled horn,

That tossed the dog,

That worried the cat,

That killed the rat,

That ate the malt,

That lay in the house that Jack built.

This is the priest all shaven and shorn

That married the man all tattered and torn,

That kissed the maiden all forlorn,

That milked the cow with the crumpled horn,

That tossed the dog,

That worried the cat,

That killed the rat,

That ate the malt,

That lay in the house that Jack built.

# The Hare and the Turtle

There was once a hare who always boasted about how fast he could run.

"I am the fastest animal in the forest," he said.

No one offered to race him until the turtle spoke up.

"I will race you," he said in his slow turtle voice.

"You!" The hare laughed. "You are the slowest animal of all."

All the animals gathered to watch the race.

The hare bounded forward, leaving the turtle in a cloud of dust.

Soon the hare looked back. The turtle was so far behind that the hare couldn't see him.

"I will just sit down and rest," said the hare. "I will easily win, even if I rest awhile."

But resting made the hare sleepy. His eyes slowly closed, and he fell asleep.

The turtle crawled past the hare without a sound.

When the hare awoke, the turtle was plodding patiently across the finish line.

The hare did not boast about his speed again—at least not for a very long time.

# Little Red Riding Hood

Once upon a time, there was a little girl everyone called Little Red Riding Hood. One day her mother gave her a basket packed with homemade bread and soup.

"I want you to take this food to your grandmother because she is ill," she said. "Now go straight along the path through the woods, and do not talk to any strangers."

Little Red Riding Hood started on her way to Grandmother's house. Soon she met a wolf.

"Good morning, Little Red Riding Hood. Where are you going this fine day?" asked the wolf.

"I am going to Grandmother's house to give her some bread and soup because she is ill," said Little Red Riding Hood.

"And where does she live?" asked the wolf.

"Deep in the woods, at the end of the path," said Little Red Riding Hood.

"You should pick some flowers to cheer her," said the wolf.

"Yes, I will," said Little Red Riding Hood.

She skipped along the path until she found some wildflowers. She ran here and there, gathering them.

Meanwhile, the wolf ran straight to Grandmother's house and gulped the old woman down.

Then he pulled on her nightgown and cap, and crawled into her bed.

When Little Red Riding Hood knocked on the door, he drew the bed covers up to his chin.

"Lift the latch and come right in," he called in his softest voice.

Little Red Riding Hood opened the door and came in.

"I have brought you bread and soup, Grandmother," she said.

"Come closer, my dear," said the wolf.

Little Red Riding Hood walked closer. "Oh, Grandmother," she said, "what big ears you have!"

"The better to hear you with, my dear."

"Oh, Grandmother, what big eyes you have!"

"The better to see you with, my dear."

"Oh, Grandmother, what big teeth you have!"

"The better to EAT you with!" snapped the wolf. And he jumped out of bed and gulped down Little Red Riding Hood.

Then the wolf fell asleep in Grandmother's bed.

His loud snoring could be heard by a woodcutter who was passing the cottage.

"That does not sound like the old woman," said the woodcutter. "I must see who it is."

He stepped into Grandmother's cottage and saw the sleeping wolf.

Quickly the woodcutter cut the wolf with his axe, and out jumped Little Red Riding Hood and her grandmother, safe and sound.

## Henny-Penny

One day an acorn fell on Henny-Penny's head.

"The sky is falling," she cried. "I must go and tell the king."

On her way to the king, she met Cocky-Locky.

"Where are you going?" asked Cocky-Locky.

"I am going to tell the king the sky is falling," said Henny-Penny. "You come too."

So Henny-Penny and Cocky-Locky hurried on together.

Soon they came to Ducky-Daddles.

"Where are you going?" asked Ducky-Daddles.

"We are going to tell the king the sky is falling," said Cocky-Locky. "You come too."

So Ducky-Daddles, Cocky-Locky, and Henny-Penny hurried along together.

They went along and went along until they met Goosey-Poosey.

"Where are you going?" asked Goosey-Poosey.

"Oh, the sky is falling. We are going to tell the king," said Ducky-Daddles. "You come too."

So they all went along together until they met Turkey-Lurkey, who also agreed to join them.

Now Henny-Penny, Cocky-Locky, Ducky-Daddles, Goosey-Poosey, and Turkey-Lurkey walked along and walked along until they met Foxy-Woxy.

"And where are you going?" asked Foxy-Woxy.

"We are going to tell the king the sky is falling," said Henny-Penny.

"But you are going the wrong way," said Foxy-Woxy. "Shall I show you the right way?"

"Yes," said Henny-Penny, Cocky-Locky, Ducky-Daddles, Goosey-Poosey, and Turkey-Lurkey.

They followed Foxy-Woxy straight to a dark cave.

"Follow me," said Foxy-Woxy. His sly yellow eyes were bright.

Turkey-Lurkey went in first.

Then Goosey-Poosey went in.

Then Ducky-Daddles and Cocky-Locky went in.

Henny-Penny was about to follow when she heard Cocky-Locky crow, "Cock-a-doodle-do!"

"My goodness," said Henny-Penny. "It must be time for me to lay an egg."

So Henny-Penny turned and rushed back home, while Foxy-Woxy and his family enjoyed a fine meal.

## The Wind and the Sun

One day the Wind and the Sun began to argue.

"I am the strongest," said the Wind.

"No, I am the strongest," said the Sun.

This argument went on and on until they decided to put the matter to a test.

"Look at that man walking down the road," said the Sun. "Let us see which of us can throw off his cape."

"It is no contest. I will easily win," said the Wind. And he began to blow and blow.

The harder he blew, the colder it grew. And the colder it grew, the more the man would hug the cape around himself. At last the Wind gave up.

The Sun smiled and began to grow warmer and warmer.

The man stopped hugging the cape around himself and let it flap about his shoulders. Then, as the Sun grew warmer and warmer, the man threw it off altogether.

The Sun had won with gentleness what the Wind could not win with force.

# The Three Billy Goats Gruff

Once there were three billy goats who were all named Gruff.

They wanted to go up a hillside to eat grass and grow fat. But to reach the hillside, they had to cross a bridge. And under the bridge, in the stream, lived a terrible troll with eyes as big as plates and a nose as long as a poker.

One day the smallest billy goat Gruff crossed the bridge.

*Trip, trap, trip, trap, trip, trap* sounded his little hooves on the bridge.

"Who is that tripping over my bridge?" roared the troll.

"It is only I," said the smallest billy goat Gruff. "I am going up to the hillside to eat and grow fat."

"I am going to eat you up," said the troll.

"No, please do not eat me. I am so small. Wait for my bigger brother. He will make a better meal for you."

"Well, be off then," said the troll.

Later the second biggest billy goat Gruff passed over the bridge.

*Trip, Trap, Trip, Trap, Trip, Trap* went his hooves on the bridge.

"Who is that tripping over my bridge?" roared the troll.

"Oh, it is I," said the second biggest billy goat Gruff. "I am going up to the hillside to eat and grow fat."

"I am going to eat you up," said the troll.

"Oh, please don't. Wait until the big billy goat Gruff comes. He is larger than I. He will make a better meal."

"Very well," said the troll.

Just then the big billy goat Gruff came along.

TRIP, TRAP, TRIP, TRAP, TRIP, TRAP went his hooves on the bridge, which shook with his weight.

"Who is that tramping over my bridge?" roared the troll.

"It is I, the big billy goat Gruff," he said in his deep voice.

"Now I am coming to eat you up," roared the troll.

"Then come! I have two spears to stick you with!"

And that is just what the billy goat did with his great, sharp horns.

And the troll was never seen again.

As for the three billy goats Gruff, they climbed the hillside and ate and grew fat.

# The Little Red Hen

There was once a pig, a duck, a cat, and a little red hen who lived together in a cozy little house.

One day the little red hen found a grain of wheat.

"Who will plant this grain of wheat?" she asked.

"Not I," grunted the pig.

"Not I," quacked the duck.

"Not I," purred the cat.

"Then I will," said the little red hen.

And she did.

The grain of wheat sprouted and grew. Soon it was tall and golden ripe.

"Who will cut the wheat?" asked the little red hen.

"Not I," grunted the pig.

"Not I," quacked the duck.

"Not I," purred the cat.

"Then I will," said the little red hen.

And she did.

Soon the wheat was ready to be ground into flour.

"Who will take the wheat to the mill?" asked the little red hen.

"Not I," grunted the pig.

"Not I," quacked the duck.

"Not I," purred the cat.

"Then I will," said the little red hen.

And she did.

When the sack of flour came back from the mill, the little red hen marched to her friends.

"Who will make the flour into bread?" she asked.

"Not I," grunted the pig.

"Not I," quacked the duck.

"Not I," purred the cat.

"Then I will," said the little red hen.

And she did.

The bread came from the oven, golden brown.

The pig, the duck, and the cat smelled fresh bread. They pushed and shoved and tumbled through the kitchen door.

"Who will eat this bread?" asked the little red hen.

"I will," grunted the pig.

"I will," quacked the duck.

"I will," purred the cat.

"No! *I* will eat it myself!" said the little red hen.

And she did.

# The Three Little Pigs

Once upon a time, there was a mother sow who had three little pigs.

One day she sent the little pigs into the world to make their fortunes.

Each pig took a different road.

The first little pig met a man with a load of straw.

"Please, sir," said the little pig, "give me some straw to build a house."

The man gave him the straw, and the little pig built a straw house.

No sooner was the little pig settled in his house than a wicked
wolf came along.

"Little pig, little pig, let me come in," he said.

"No, not by the hair of my chinny, chin, chin!" answered the
little pig.

"If you don't," said the wolf, "I'll huff and I'll puff, and I'll
blow your house in!"

But the little pig wouldn't open the door.

So the wolf huffed and he puffed, and he blew the house in.
And he ate the first little pig.

Now, the second little pig met a man with a bundle of sticks.

"Please, sir," he said, "give me some sticks to build a house."

The man did, and the little pig built a house with the sticks.

Then along came the wolf. He knocked at the door and said, "Little pig, little pig, let me come in."

And the little pig answered, "No, not by the hair of my chinny, chin, chin!"

"If you don't," said the wolf, "I'll huff and I'll puff, and I'll blow your house in!"

But the little pig wouldn't open the door.

So the wolf huffed and he puffed, and he blew the house in. And he ate the second little pig.

Now, the third little pig met a man with a load of bricks.

"Please, sir," he said, "give me some bricks to build a house."

The man did, and the pig built a strong brick house.

Then the wolf came and knocked on the door and said, "Little pig, little pig, let me come in."

"No, not by the hair of my chinny, chin, chin!" answered the little pig.

"If you don't," said the wolf, "I'll huff and I'll puff, and I'll blow your house in!"

But the little pig wouldn't open the door.

So the wolf huffed and he puffed, and he puffed and he huffed, but he couldn't blow the house in.

So the wolf leaped onto the little pig's roof.

"I am going to come down your chimney and eat you up," he roared.

Quickly the little pig lit a fire under the pot in his fireplace.

The water was already boiling when the wolf landed with a splash. The little pig clapped the lid on the pot, and that was the end of the wolf.

And the third little pig lived happily ever after.

## The Lion and the Mouse

Once a lion lay sleeping.

A mouse ran across his paw.

The lion woke up and roared and grabbed the mouse.

"Please, Lion, do not hurt me. I am sorry I woke you, but if you do not hurt me, I promise I will do something good for you someday."

"Ha!" laughed the lion. "What could a tiny mouse do for a big strong lion?"

But all the same, the lion let the mouse go.